Hobart

Hobart

by Anita Briggs

illustrated by Mary Rayner

SIMON & SCHUSTER BOOKS FOR YOUNG READERS

New York London Toronto Sydney Singapore

SIMON & SCHUSTER BOOKS FOR YOUNG READERS
An imprint of Simon & Schuster Children's Publishing Division
1230 Avenue of the Americas, New York, New York 10020

Book design by Mark Siegel
The text of this book is set in Goudy Old Style.
Printed in the United States of America
10 9 8 7 6 5 4 3 2 1

Library of Congress Cataloging-in-Publication Data
Briggs, Anita. Hobart / by Anita Briggs ; illustrated by Mary
Rayner.
p. cm. Summary: Four budding artists, a tap dancer, a poet, a
singer, and an acrobat, who just happen to be pigs, live out their
dreams and avoid becoming bacon.
ISBN 0-689-84129-9 [1. Pigs—Fiction. 2. Farm life—Fiction.
3. Domestic animals—Fiction. 4. Hope—Fiction.] I. Rayner,
Mary, ill. II. Title. PZ7.B76425Ho 2002 [Fic]—dc21 00-052256

*I*n grateful memory of Phoebe Mizell, my fifth-grade teacher, who inspired us with the love of literature and a longing for adventure—A. B.

Pigs in Peril

Hobart was a pig. Just to look at him, you wouldn't think he was so very different from his brothers, Byron and Wilfred, and his sister, Violet.

They were all round, pink, and quite clean. This was because they belonged to a good farmer. They lived in a grassy meadow with a stream and a pond to play in, so they didn't have to wallow in the mud.

Watching them as they nuzzled one another fondly, or sipped buttermilk from the trough, you might be tempted to say, "Those pigs are all alike!"

But you would be wrong. Hobart was different. Hobart was a hopeful pig. No one seemed to know why Hobart was hopeful, or how he got that way. He had always been hopeful, all through both years of his life.

Byron wanted to be a poet and recite his verses to an audience, but he couldn't make the lines come out even. He had been practicing, though, right up to the day when he absentmindedly nibbled at some of the old gander's grain.

Now, the gander was the terror of the farmyard because of his evil temper. All the smaller animals kept their distance from him, for he hissed, pecked, and pinched at anything within reach.

As he watched Farmer Mills' growing fondness for the little pink pigs, he became even more spiteful. He raged when he saw choice bits of food from the farmhouse put into their trough instead of his. He grew sick and tired of seeing the pampered Byron standing on a tub, waving his arms and dramatically declaiming his fractured verses. And now the young hog was stealing his food! The gander rushed at Byron in a fury, head low and wings flapping.

"You'll be eaten, you know," he screeched. "You and your brothers and your sister, too!" He slid to a halt, his head snaking from side to side, and his voice dropped to a sinister whisper. "You know, Byron, you'll make a very tasty side of bacon, and quite a few crispy cutlets, too. Best of all, I won't have to listen to your tiresome poems when you're sizzling in a frying pan."

Byron's eyes grew wide with horror. Then he crept slowly away, whispering:

> "What's the use of having fun?
> Sweet the corn and warm the sun,
> But soon my young life will be done.
> I'll be a side of bacon."

Hobart, eating hot mash, heard Byron's verse and saw the tears streaming down his snout. "Cheer up, Byron!" he said, nuzzling his brother gently. "That grumpy old goose is making up silly stories to scare you. He doesn't mean it! He's just cross because you ate his grain." Then he scampered off to hunt for acorns.

But Byron would not cheer up. After that, he stopped trying to improve his skills as a poet.

Byron was not the only gifted pig in the

family. Little Violet, in her first year of life, had exhibited remarkable talent as an acrobat, landing squarely on her feet after an accidental somersault from the loft. Since then she had learned to do a back flip and was working bravely at standing on her snout. Wilfred, with his big barrel chest, had been born with a beautiful tenor

voice. Once, a pair of skylarks nesting in the eaves of the barn had exclaimed over his singing, calling it "promising."

Violet and Wilfred worked hard at developing their talents until one crisp afternoon when Farmer Mills let a new cow into the barnyard. She was sleek and golden and wore a red leather collar with a brass bell. She tossed her head and made the bell chime as she strolled past Violet and Wilfred, who were sipping buttermilk from a shiny metal tub. They looked up with friendly eyes.

"Hello there, pork chops," she mooed, looking down her long nose.

Violet and Wilfred stared in shocked silence.

"Oh, didn't you know? That's what all pigs come to, in the end. On the other hand, *I* am a milk-cow. I'm far too valuable alive to be turned into a steak."

Violet burst into tears, and Wilfred turned away, trembling.

"What are you complaining about, you stupid swine?" asked the cow, switching her tail irritably. "You don't know how lucky you are. Where I come from, pigs live in the mud. They drink stale water and sleep in dirty straw. As to what they eat, I refuse to think about that." She gave a delicate shudder. "My kind are treated very differently, of course; fresh hay, stalls washed down every day. But, after all, we're important—*we* are the milk-givers, you know." She looked around the cobbled yard. "You should count your blessings. You seem to have a good life here—for as long as it lasts, that is. You *are* only pigs, after all."

Hobart came upon Violet lying despondently

on her side, weeping quietly as Wilfred crooned a mournful tune. He tried to rally them, saying, "What's wrong with everybody around here? First Byron, and now you two! You shouldn't be jealous of that conceited milk machine. She *is* very pretty, but Farmer Mills will love us just the same, you'll see!" Then Hobart, sure that he had comforted his sister and brother, trotted happily away to dig for roots.

"What's the use of trying to explain to Hobart?" cried Violet. "He'll never believe anything bad."

"What's the use of *anything*?" sighed Wilfred drearily. "Why should I work myself to the bone on scales and breathing exercises and diction, when everybody knows I'll end up between two slices of bread? Then who's going to say, 'My, but that sandwich has a beautiful tenor voice!'?" He heaved a deep sigh, then flopped down and lay on his side too.

"You're right," Violet wept. "I'm not going to spend my time practicing acrobatics just so I can somersault into a sausage machine." Byron, who had been gazing moodily at the trough, came shuffling over and joined them on the ground.

Mrs. Mills came out to feed the chickens, and saw Wilfred, Violet, and Byron lying there. "Hen-RY!" she called. "Come on out here. These poor pigs don't look right."

Farmer Mills came running from the house and bent over to look at them. "Poor Byron," he said. "Poor little Violet." He stroked her head gently. "What's the matter, Wilfred? Are you sick? Hobart, now, he looks healthy enough."

"Hurry back to the house, Henry, and bring me some of that rosemary-dandelion tonic. That'll fix them up, right as rain," said Mrs. Mills.

The pigs didn't mind taking the tonic, because it tasted deliciously sweet. But

when the nice taste had faded away, Wilfred had an unwelcome thought. "Great," he grumbled dejectedly. "Now we'll be rosemary-flavored pork chops."

And so it came about that Violet and Wilfred and Byron gave up their ambitions for a life upon the stage.

Hobart alone refused to face up to his fate. He shook his head in puzzlement when he saw how gloomy the others were. He just didn't believe such a dreadful end was coming for them, for Hobart was always hopeful. Besides, he could think of little else but his secret ambition. He dreamed day and night of what he longed for more than acorn squash or corn bread; more, even, than buttermilk. Hobart wanted, more than anything in the world, to tap-dance.

Hobart's Dream

$\mathcal{H}$obart's dream had begun one evening in the past summer when he wandered close to Farmer Mills' house and heard a lovely clicking sound through the open parlor window. Standing on his hind feet, he peered in and saw Mrs. Mills, the farmer's wife, rocking and knitting, her eyes

fixed on a flickering screen. There on the
television was a little curly-haired girl
dancing around a ship's deck. Her feet were
tapping so fast that Hobart's eyes could
scarcely follow them. Her curls bounced,
and she had a bright smile on her face.

Hobart was enchanted. How happy he
would be if only he could dance like that
little girl! He shuffled merrily about in the
flower bed beneath the window, making
Mrs. Mills' daisies and petunias fly right
and left. But after a few moments he
stopped. His feet weren't making the same
sounds that the little girl's feet had made—
beautiful crispy sounds, like beechnuts
when he cracked them in his teeth.
Something was missing, but he didn't know
what. He watched for a little while longer
and then went back to the barn to think.

The next morning, while rooting for a

snack in the soft ground under the beech tree, Hobart found two old bottle caps. He looked at them for a long time. Then he fitted them carefully to his hind feet and tried a few of the steps he'd seen through the parlor window.

To his disappointment, his feet still didn't make the nice noise he'd heard on the television. So he sat down under the tree and tried to remember what he'd seen. The little girl hadn't been dancing in the dirt. She'd been tapping on a ship's deck! So Hobart, always hopeful, trotted over to the loading dock in front of the barn.

Hop-shuffle-step, hop-shuffle-step went Hobart, exactly like the curly haired girl, and there! Just like magic, there was that lovely sound. *Clickety-click! Clickety-click!*

Then he had an idea. The little girl had

only two feet, but Hobart had four. Wasn't that even better? He ran back to the beech tree as fast as he could go. He put his pink snout into the earth around its base and rooted. He rooted on the north side of the tree, then moved around to the south and tried again. And there, shining underneath the loose dirt, were two more bottle caps.

Hobart stepped into them with his front feet and loped back to the barn. *Clickety-click click click! Clickety-click click click!* Why, this was twice as good as the curly haired girl! And if he moved gracefully sideways, swinging his head

jauntily to the beat while tapping on all fours . . . *clickety-click—CRASH!*

Unfortunately he had fallen over his own left hind foot. But Hobart was always hopeful. Picking himself up, he dusted straw from his hindquarters. "Practice!" he cried happily. "That's all I need, more practice. Then people will come from miles around to watch me. 'Just look at that pig!' they'll say. 'He's a tap-dancing fool.'"

And so Hobart's dream was born.

A Desperate Business

One night, a week after the new cow had arrived, Hobart, Byron, Violet, and Wilfred lay in a circle on the barn floor. Though it was late, they were wide awake. Moonbeams shone through a cobwebbed window onto the hay.

"Did you see it?" asked Violet, her little eyes glistening with tears in the silvery light. "That big truck that drove in today? And the man with the loud voice who got out and talked with Farmer Mills? Farmer Mills looked sad. 'I wish I'd never thought of raising a litter of pigs,' he said. 'I didn't know how hard this was going to be. But I do have to pay the bills.' Then he told the loud man he'd leave a note in his mailbox tomorrow morning. There's no doubt about it, our days are numbered."

"What truck?" asked Hobart. "I didn't see any truck."

"That's because you were tap-dancing," explained Wilfred patiently. "And I must say you looked very promising, Hobart. Not that you'll have any use for that sort of thing in the future. Who ever heard of a bunch of pickled pigs' feet tapping their way across a meat counter?"

"The truck was big," recited Byron slowly and dreamily.
"A painted pig
In red and white
Stood on its right.
The letters spelled
'City Meat Co., Wholesale and Retail.'"

"Arrgh!" he squealed. "It NEVER comes out right!"

" 'Processed to Your Specification. Custom Cut and Wrapped,'" added Wilfred glumly.

" 'Choice Corn-fed Pork. Sausage. Bacon. Baked Glazed Hams by Special Order,'" continued Violet, her voice breaking.

Hobart leaped to his feet, his eyes
horrified. "WAIT A MINUTE. Are you
telling me that WE are PORK?"

Violet nodded. "We've been trying to
tell you for days. We were wondering when
you were going to wake up to Life, Hobart."

"But—we're—we're ARTISTS!" Hobart protested. "They can't eat artists!"

"Artists today, picnic hams tomorrow," muttered Wilfred.

"Never." Hobart took a deep breath and spoke firmly. "This must NEVER be. It would be a dreadful loss to the world. We'll—we'll just PROVE ourselves," he continued in a more cheerful voice. "When they see what talented artists we are, they'll never think of grinding us up for sausage." He sat back down on the straw, trying not to shiver.

"But we're not ready!" Byron cried.

"Wilfred has a fine singing voice, but he doesn't know any songs. You trip over your own feet when you tap-dance. Violet still falls down two out of three times when she tries to spin around on her snout. And as for my poetry—well, there's always at least one line left over."

"Time," said Hobart hopefully. "That's all we need . . . time. Time to practice our acts."

"How do WE know how much time we have?" asked Violet. "The City Meat truck could carry us off any day!"

"She's right," said Wilfred with a sigh. "There's nothing we can do but wait to be made into bacon."

"Dig," said Hobart.

They looked at him in bewilderment.

"*Dig!*" he repeated, louder this time.

"We'll dig our way out under the fence. Come on, let's get going!" He lurched to his feet and dashed for the barn door.

As they crossed the barnyard the lights went on in the parlor. The pigs halted, then crept cautiously up to the window. Farmer Mills was pacing slowly back and forth across the room, his head bowed. As they watched he sat down at his desk, drew a sheet of paper from the drawer, and began to write.

"Poor Farmer Mills," whispered Violet. "He can't sleep. See how worried he looks? He's writing that note. That means the truck might be coming tomorrow!"

"You mean today," Hobart said as the stable clock chimed midnight. "What if he hears us and comes out to investigate? Hurry up, everybody, and don't make a sound!"

Fearfully the four pigs tiptoed past the house, around the chicken shed, and out to the fence in the meadow.

"We'll dig here, by the beech tree, where the ground's soft," said Hobart.

Through the darkness under the tree came sounds of snuffling and rooting, and then a crunch as Wilfred cracked a juicy beechnut between his strong, white teeth.

"Stop that noise, Wilfred!
I hear your molars crunch!
This is desperate business.
We have no time for lunch!"

Hobart and Violet looked at Byron with awe.

"That's *much* better, Byron," said Violet. "It came out right that time, didn't it?"

"As a matter of fact, it did," Byron murmured, looking modestly down at his toes. "Though properly it should have said dinner . . . no, breakfast, now. If I had more time, I could polish the rhyme—"

"Later," whispered Hobart. "Dig for your life! That snoopy gander must have heard us, and now he's coming up the path! If he sees what we're up to, he'll start squawking his head off, and then we *will* be sausage."

Dirt flew from four pink snouts as the hole under the fence grew wider and deeper.

"There!" cried Hobart. "That ought to do it. You go first, Violet, and hurry!"

Violet dived quickly into the hole, did a rolling turn, and scrambled to her feet on the other side of the fence. Byron and Hobart followed, but when it was Wilfred's turn, he got stuck halfway under and couldn't move.

The gander waddled into view, his feathers gleaming in the moonlight. He was beating his wings and screaming a furious warning now, his beak pointed to the fading stars. The farm dogs began to stir and growl. Then one of them barked sharply, and a screen door slammed.

"Come on, Wilfred," urged Byron desperately. "You can make it!"

Now they heard the dogs barking hysterically.

"It's my rib cage!" Wilfred moaned. "It's too big. Go on without me, or you'll all be caught!"

"Ah!" cried Hobart. "Good! A big rib cage—the mark of a great singer! Dig, everybody, dig!"

In a moment Wilfred was free, and the four pigs were scurrying into the shelter of the woods as fast as their legs would carry them.

The Distant Hills

*H*obart led the others through the woods and up a little stream. But they weren't used to running so far, and soon they fell to the ground, struggling for breath.

"We'll never get away in time," wailed Wilfred.

"You're right," mourned Byron, clutching at a stitch in his side. "I think the dogs are gaining on us. It's all because of that spiteful gander! He'd love for us to be popped into an oven."

"Even if we do manage to escape them," said Violet, "what's the use? There won't be anything to eat in the woods."

"Of course we'll escape!" cried Hobart. "The dogs can't follow our tracks, because we ran in the stream. We'll just go on until we find a good place to set up for our practice. There'll be plenty of nuts and things. But we can't stay here. Get up now! And run like you've never run before!"

So the four pigs ran and ran all through the dark night until their weary legs would take them no farther.

At last they stopped, too tired to take another step. Then they looked around them in wonder. The first rays of the sun shone on a small hill rising above them. It was crowned with craggy stones, and it

seemed a magical place to the young pigs, who had never been outside the fence before.

"Perfect!" panted Hobart. They all lay gasping in the soft grass. "This is the perfect spot for us! Violet can do her flips from the top of the rocks, and somersault all the way down the hill. Wilfred can practice singing as loudly as he wants—there's nobody around to hear. Byron can make up poems about the beautiful trees and rocks and sky, and as for me"—Hobart pointed to a large, flat slab of rock near the base of the hill— "why, it's the ideal place to work on my tap dancing!"

The weeks went by, and never were four pigs busier or happier. The bright leaves fell from the oak and beech trees. Winter came, and snow drifted lightly

from the sky, yet the pigs slept snug and
warm, curled together on the dried grass
in the shelter of the crags. They ate
acorns and beechnuts from the forest and
drank from the sparkling stream that
wound around the base of the hill. But
mostly they practiced. Day and night,
they practiced being artists.

They made colorful costumes from
fallen leaves, red berries, and yellow
grasses. Byron searched his mind for
words that rhymed, like *should* and *good*
and *corn* and *born*. Wilfred worked on

singing a high C so clear and strong that it shattered the icicles hanging from the rocks. And the sound of Hobart's tapping feet was heard from sunrise to sunset.

"We're getting thinner," he said proudly as he tightened his belt one morning in late winter. "It's all this exercise, and no trough to eat from. We wouldn't be any good to Farmer Mills now, even if we went back to the farm."

"That reminds me," said Byron with grave importance. "There's something I've been meaning to say."

Everyone gathered around curiously.
Byron cleared his throat.

"*Farmer Mills was kind and good,*"
he began.
"*He fed us as a farmer should.*
On milk and cabbages and corn
We fattened since we first were born.
We wallowed not in mud and mire
Nor lay within a mucky byre,
But bathed in water clear and sweet
And slept in soft straw, clean and neat.
He raised us for a purpose high:
For corn-fed pork! Though we must die
We owe him—we owe him—er,
we owe—"

Loud cries of protest interrupted Byron's
verse.

"Are you CRAZY?" yelped Wilfred.

"Give up our art, and our lives, to pay Farmer Mills' bills? Speak for yourself. Maybe pig poets are a dime a dozen, but who ever heard a pork chop do THIS?"

He took a deep breath, expanded his chest, and hit a high C. There was a faint

tinkling sound as icicles splintered and fell from the rocks.

"Wow!" Violet exclaimed. "Beautiful! Wilfred, all that practice has really done the trick. Now, if you only knew some songs."

"I know lots of *tunes*," Wilfred said a bit huffily. Then he hung his head in embarrassment. "Tunes come into my head all the time, but I can't do the words, somehow. And even though my voice is strong and clear enough to break icicles, no one's going to pay me just to sing, 'AHHH!'"

Another icicle fell to the ground.

"Lyrics," said Hobart.

"What?" asked Wilfred.

"Lyrics. That's what you need. Lyrics are words that you sing. They're poems, really, set to music. And poems are what Byron does."

"A poet is the conscience of his nation," Byron objected. "I can't waste my time on silly songs. I know what they're like. 'Moon, June; love, dove,' for goodness' sake. Besides, we have an issue before us. We do owe *something* to Farmer Mills, don't we? Even if we end up as bacon, we've had a better life than most pigs!"

"That's it!" cried Hobart, his voice ringing with hope. "Wilfred, you sing Byron's lyrics— er, poem—to one of your tunes. But first, Violet, you introduce the song. Do a half gainer from the top of the rocks, somersault down the slope, and announce the act. We'll pay our dues to Farmer Mills and stay out of the frying pan as well!"

"Hobart," Wilfred said slowly, "I believe

you've got it!"

Violet climbed onto the topmost rock,
dived off in a
graceful half gainer,
did a fine
somersault, and hit
her head against a
stone. Her brothers
rushed to her aid.

"I'll be all right
in a minute," she
said, opening one
eye. "I just need a
little more
practice."

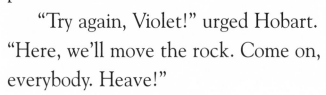

"Try again, Violet!" urged Hobart.
"Here, we'll move the rock. Come on,
everybody. Heave!"

A Narrow Escape

The sun was warm, and daffodils were pushing green spears through the grass when the pigs trotted merrily down the highway on their way to the farm. They were full of excitement. Their act was perfect, and they could hardly wait to show Farmer Mills.

But suddenly there was a terrible roaring noise. A huge truck came speeding around a bend in the road. A red and white pig was painted on its side, and large letters spelled out CITY MEAT CO., WHOLESALE AND RETAIL.

"Hide!" cried Hobart, diving for some bushes. But it was too late. The truck's brakes squealed, and a large, red-faced man jumped out.

"Aha!" he said. "Just what I need—free pork chops! They look a little stringy, but I'll soon fatten them up."

"We'll have to run for it!" gasped Hobart. And run they did, but the man's legs were much longer than theirs, and by the time they reached the bank of the river he had almost caught up with them.

"Somebody think of something," pleaded Byron, "or we'll all be turned into lunch meat."

"Oh no, we won't!" Hobart said as he

jammed his bottle caps onto his feet and launched into a rapid double shuffle. The man stopped short, his mouth hanging open.

Hobart nodded to Violet, and with a desperate effort, she flung herself through the air in a double back flip. "Circus pigs," the man whispered faintly, and staggered a bit.

At that very moment Wilfred hit an earsplitting high C. The man clapped his hands to his head, stumbled backward, and

fell moaning into the river. As he floated
downstream, clinging to a log, Byron cried,

> "Unhappy man! Such direful deeds
> A shameful fate must bring!
> May roaring waters cover you—cover
> you—cover you—

"Oh, bother the rhymes! Brute! Thief!
Pig-napper!"

The pigs scurried over the bridge and
across the meadow to the farmhouse. There
they paused on the porch, looking at one
another in silence. Then Hobart took a

deep breath and rapped the knocker. They
heard slow steps, and Farmer
Mills opened the door. When
he saw the pigs, his eyes
opened wide in surprise.

Hobart began
in a rush, his words
tumbling over one
another.

"Farmer Mills, we're
sorry if we caused you trouble, but you see,
we didn't want to be made into pork chops.
We've been practicing very hard, and we
hope we can be useful to you in another
way. What would you think of 'Farmer
Mills' Performing Pigs'? Would you like to
see our act? I can tap-dance, and Violet is
an acrobat, and Wilfred sings, and Byron
recites poetry . . . "

Just then there was a sloshing noise as the truck man stamped into the yard, water streaming from his clothes. "Ah, Farmer Mills!" he said with a wide smile. "I came to ask if you'd seen my circus pigs. I see they've fetched up at your house, probably looking for me. They have a special performance tonight, so I'll just take them off your hands."

Farmer Mills made himself very tall, and looked at the man with stern eyes. "These are *my* pigs, as you know very well, you sausage grinder. And I told you, before they—er—went on vacation, that I'd changed my mind about selling them to you. They're all going to live to a ripe old age, right here on my farm."

The truck man's face turned even redder with fury. "Sausage grinder, am I?"

he shouted. "Well, let me tell you, you'll soon get tired of feeding those four greedy hogs! Pig hugger! Swine lover!" He took a wild swing at the farmer.

But Farmer Mills gave him a push, and he tumbled down the step and landed sprawling on the grass. "You have exactly ten seconds to get off my property, you lowdown thief," said Farmer Mills, "and don't let me ever see your red face on this farm again."

As the truck man scurried off, muttering and dripping,

Farmer Mills turned to the pigs. "Brave Hobart! And dear little Violet. And Byron and Wilfred—my, my." He shook his head and wiped his eyes with a bandanna handkerchief. "Farmer Mills' Performing Pigs, eh? Yes, I like it very much. Now, show me your act. But first, tell me how in the world you managed to think of such a thing. And how ever did you escape the City Meat truck?"

"It was Hobart," said Byron. "He never gave up hope."

Home Again, Home Again

$\mathcal{S}$pring had come to the valley. In Farmer Mills' barnyard an audience sat in chairs under the flowering apple trees. Everyone was breathless with excitement. Mrs. Mills handed out glasses of lemonade. Farmer Mills, a happy smile on his face, passed his straw hat down the rows. Little Mary Alice Brown dropped a quarter into the hat. Old Mrs. Woodworth added a pair of newly knitted red socks. And Dr. Noble, the veterinarian, put in three whole dollars.

Byron, standing in front of the barn, banged two pans together as Violet appeared in the loft door, did a triple airborne somersault, and landed neatly on her feet in the deep straw.

"Ladies and gentlemen!" cried Hobart over the loud cheers. "Permit me to introduce the Performing Pigs: Violet, Wilfred, Byron, and myself—Hobart. Violet is our acrobat, and Wilfred is our singer. Byron, our poet, wrote the lyrics for this show, and I am a tap dancer. And now—let the music begin!"

Wilfred stepped out of the barn, bowed, inhaled deeply, and started to sing.

"*Farmer Mills was kind and good;*
He fed us as a farmer should."

Byron hit the pans together gently to keep the beat.

"*On milk and cabbages and corn*
We fattened since we first were born."

Wilfred was singing such a beautiful melody that the listeners felt tears gathering in their eyes. Then the tempo picked up. Violet took a few sycamore balls out of her beech-leaf pouch and began to juggle, doing an occasional back flip.

"*We wallowed NOT in mud and mire*
Nor lay within a mucky byre," sang Wilfred, more dramatically.

Hobart stepped quietly out upon the bricks, slipping into an elegant tap dance.

*"But bathed in water clear and sweet
And slept in soft straw, clean and neat."*

Byron began to harmonize softly.

"He raised us for a purpose high!"
declared Wilfred.
"Performing Pigs! We cannot lie . . ."

Little Mary Alice Brown and Dr. Noble

were tapping their feet and nodding their heads in time to the music.

> *"We ran away to try our skills;*
> *We practiced in the distant hills.*
> *But now we're back to pay the bills!*
> *Hooray for kindly Farmer Mills!"*

The music was growing still louder. Violet's sycamore balls flashed through the air as she stood confidently upon her snout. Hobart shifted into a double shuffle, turning in graceful circles.

> *"When that Pig-napper would have tossed*
> *Us in his truck, and all seemed lost,*
> *Our Hobart donned his bottle caps*
> *And stunned him with his dazzling taps!*
> *Then Violet's flips and Wilfred's scream*
> *Made him fall* splash! *into the stream."*

Wilfred's voice took on a graver tone.

"Once more he followed on our track!
But when he tried to take us back,
Our farmer threw him off the farm
And vowed we'd never come to harm."

They all joined in for the grand finale.

"They'll never pickle Hobart's feet
Or sandwich Wilfred's tenor sweet
Or glaze poor Byron's poet lips
Or process Violet's double flips."

Now everyone was applauding wildly,
Farmer Mills the loudest of all, as the artists
came to the end of their song.

"Our hopeful Hobart found the way!
Performing Pigs no more will stray.

We'll earn our keep for each new day
And dance and sing your cares away!"

And the Performing Pigs lived happily
ever after, with time off in the hills each
winter to learn new acts. Farmer Mills
became a prosperous man, and the City
Meat truck never came again.

We'll earn our keep for each new day
And dance and sing your cares away!"

And the Performing Pigs lived happily ever after, with time off in the hills each winter to learn new acts. Farmer Mills became a prosperous man, and the City Meat truck never came again.